A Very Merry Christmas

A Very Merry Christmas

by Maudie Powell-Tuck ★ Illustrated by Gill Guile

SCHOLASTIC INC.

It was Christmas Eve at Bramble Cottage,
and everything looked perfect.
Ornaments sparkled on the tree,
and decorations hung on the fireplace.

But something was missing.
"It just doesn't feel like
Christmas," sighed Mr. Mouse.

"I know what we need," said Mrs. Mouse. "A Christmas party!"

So they put on their boots and scurried off to invite their friends.

There was just time to bake
some cookies before they heard
a KNOCK! KNOCK! KNOCK!
at the door.

"Merry Christmas!" cried Fox.
"Look what I've made. You can't
have Christmas without
a dinosaur cake!"

"What a good idea!" said
Mrs. Mouse.

"Dinosaur cake at Christmas?"
squeaked Mr. Mouse. "Are
you sure?"

Just then, there was a
RAT-A-TAT-TAT!

"We've brought our piano," said
Mr. Beaver. "Christmas just isn't
the same without beaver carols!"

"Get ready, everyone," added Mrs. Rabbit.
"Here come the kids!"

Wheeee!
In skidded six little ladybug bunnies.
"They always dress up for Christmas," smiled Mrs. Rabbit fondly.

Then Mrs. Beaver struck up a tune.
"Deck the dams with mud a-plenty,
Fa la la la la, la la la la!"
"Goodness!" squeaked Mr. Mouse.
"Are ladybugs and mud Christmassy?"

DING DONG! went
the doorbell.

"I hope I'm not too late," said Bear. "I couldn't find a big enough cactus. It's not Christmas without a cactus."

"A cactus? At Christmas?"
cried Mr. Mouse.

"Enough!"

wailed Mr. Mouse. "Cactuses, dinosaurs, and ladybugs AREN'T right! This isn't like Christmas at all!"

"But darling," said Mrs. Mouse, "everyone is having such a great time."

Mr. Mouse looked around.

Bear was dancing with the ladybug bunnies . . .

Fox had joined in with the beaver carols . . .

and Mr. Rabbit had already eaten far too much dinosaur cake.

Mr. Mouse began to smile. It was a little bit silly. It was a little bit odd. But without a doubt, it was . . .

. . . the most wonderful Christmas ever!

For Mutti Bear x ~ M. P. T.

For my wonderful husband and best friend, Andy x ~ G. G.

Originally published in Great Britain in 2014 by Little Tiger Press Ltd

ISBN 978-0-545-81242-9

Text by Maudie Powell-Tuck. Text copyright © 2014 by Little Tiger Press.
Illustrations copyright © 2014 by Gill Guile. All rights reserved.
Published by Scholastic Inc., 557 Broadway, New York, NY 10012,
by arrangement with Little Tiger Press Ltd.
SCHOLASTIC and associated logos are trademarks
and/or registered trademarks of Scholastic Inc.

12 11 10 9 8 7 6 5 4 3 2   14 15 16 17 18 19/0

Printed in the U.S.A.   40

First Scholastic printing, November 2014